Ten Tall Tales

**written and illustrated
by E.J. Bird**

 Carolrhoda Books, Inc., Minneapolis

For Robyn, my ever-lovin' daughter

LIBRARY OF CONGRESS CATALOGING IN PUBLICATION DATA

Bird, E. J.
    Ten tall tales.

    Summary: Mr. Bird presents ten Western tall
tales that he has heard throughout his life, some
of them his own.
    1. Tall tales. 2. Children's stories, American.
[1. Tall tales. 2. Short stories. 3. West (U.S.) —
Fiction] I. Title.
PZ7.B51192Te 1984   [Fic]   84-12086
ISBN 0-87614-267-6 (lib. bdg.)
 1 2 3 4 5 6 7 8 9 10 92 91 90 89 88 87 86 85 84

Contents

Foreword

Most of the many years of my life have been spent in the West. I was born just two generations removed from the time in our history when the West was still considered the Great Frontier, and our family lived very close to that frontier when I was growing up. Our rocky one-man farm was tucked into the foothills of Utah's Wasatch Mountains, east of Layton, two miles south of the Weber River. At that time there were more horse-drawn rigs on our end of the road than there were Model T Fords. Peddlers, prospectors, tinkers, drifters, all found their way to our table and spent the cool evenings on our big porch, sharing their news and their stories.

Two summers during my late teens were given to the fields and cattle of the large ranches on the upper Snake River in Idaho. I think I could still ride a worked-over bronc or harness a team for a day's work. Those nights spent in bunkhouses and around camp fires produced some tall tales told by experts.

As State Director of the Utah Federal Art Project during the Great Depression, I traveled over most of the state. It was during this time that Buck Lee wandered into my studio and into my life. Buck was a cowpuncher-artist and, without a doubt, the best all-around storyteller I have ever heard. "Old Scratch," "The Cottonwood Tree," "The Snake," and "Fast Horses" were all his tales. With a little prodding from me, two of these found their way into *Utah: A Guide to the State*, published by the Utah Federal Writer's Project.

In later years I had the good fortune to spend some time, and many camp fires, with two well-known and beloved Utahns, Dr. Dean Brimhall and Dr. Walter Cottam. It was with these men that I discovered the wild, lonesome canyons of southeastern

Utah and got a feeling for our back country and deserts.

From all these people, and from many others I have not mentioned, I have heard and collected countless tall tales. Here are ten that I have especially enjoyed over the years. Some are even my own. Now I pass them on to you.

E.J. Bird

E.J. BIRD

Old Scratch

I was comin' down off the mountain, ridin' my buckskin and leadin' a couple of pack horses, when I come upon a dead bear layin' 'longside the trail. The place was all tore up, brush busted every which-a-way and the gravel scattered like there'd been a terrible fight. I looked up, and there, hunkered high in an old pine tree, was this little black cub. Shinnyin' up the trunk, I snaked him bellerin' and clawin' all the way down. He'd been hurt. He was scratched and bleedin', and he had one ear chewed off.

Well now, I just can't ride off and leave him with his mother layin' there dead, so I hauled him back to the ranch. Fed him cow's milk and such. Raised him to be quite a sizeable bear. Figured he'd have to earn his keep, so after a couple of years, I had him broke to ride.

11

I found that ridin' a bear was some different than ridin' a horse. We'd be goin' along nice and easy when he'd stop real quick and turn over a log to look for grubs, or he'd back up to a low limb or a tree trunk and rear around to scratch his back. Lord, he was always scratchin'—guess that's why I named him Old Scratch. Another thing, he could smell a honey tree a country mile—and when he found one it was pure hell on the rider.

Anyway, he had his good points, like bein' good natured and mighty soft ridin'. And sometimes, when we was lookin' for cattle in the high country, we would climb to the top of one of those old sugar pines and see clear into the next county. Most people were right surprised, if you come upon 'em real sudden like, to see me ridin' a one-eared, saddle-broke bear.

This one day, we was high up on the mountain when we come upon this other bear. Almost before I could grab the cinch and rip off the saddle, they were at it— snarlin' and scratchin' and really tearin' each other apart. I see my bear was gettin' the worst of it, so I reach in and grab him by the hair on his back and haul him out. I get a-straddle and set the spurs to him. We get out of there fast— headin' straight down the mountain, with the other bear about six jumps behind. Well, there we was, tearin' down through the

brush, and me cussin' and hollerin' when he wouldn't stop or turn or nuthin', hangin' on for all I was worth and pullin' hair. I guess then's when I noticed it, and it was like one of those bad dreams. Lord, I looked twice just to make sure—and so help me, this bear had two good ears!

Did I ever get my own bear back? Sure, after a day and a half gatherin' up my saddle and the rest of my gear. Got him squared away and come down to a little creek, when he spies this bee tree. Boy, grab your hat! Up we went, with the bark a-flyin', the bees a-buzzin' and stingin', and me cussin' with my eyes swelled almost shut. Mad? I was so mad I hauled him down and got me a club. I smashed him so hard on the nose it crossed both his eyes! He was bellerin' when he took off up the mountain.

So, if any you fellers ever come across a one-eared, cross-eyed, saddle-broke bear, you'll know it's Old Scratch.

The Cottonwood Tree

Everybody's got his problems. I remember years ago, in the late fall, me and a couple of hands were drivin' about two hundred head of cattle down off the high country to the ranch for winter feedin'. They was full of good summer feed and feelin' a might sassy, but we was keepin' 'em bunched up and makin' pretty good time. We come to a

16

place where most times we ford the Colorado
River, but this time she was in high flood.
The water was deep and churnin' along so
fast that I knew for sure we couldn't make
it. No sense to wait it out, 'cause it might
take a week for the river to go down, and
there was nothin' but rocks, like bare bones,
for miles, and no feed for the cattle.

Well, I prowled around a little, and I
come upon this old cottonwood tree by the

E.J. BIRD

riverbank. You just can't believe how big
she was. I looked her over and pounded on
her. I found she was as holler as last year's

brown jug. Anyway, I thought I could cut her down and lay her across the river. So while I chopped on the tree, the two hands worked over the herd. Had to rope and throw twenty-seven of them big old long-horn steers and saw off their horns so's they would fit crost-wise of the tree.

After about a day and a half's work, and a lot of cussin', we started 'em through that holler cottonwood. Lost two calves that fell out a knothole, and it took us another half day to flush some of them critters out of the limbs, but we got 'em through and over the river.

If you don't believe me, I can take you there sometime and show you the old tree, if the floods ain't got her. Leastwise, you can still see the pile of horns we left layin' there among the rocks.

The Singing Coyotes

Did I ever tell you about the winter I spent out in the Cedar Flats country trappin' coyotes for bounty? It's a wild and lonesome place, but I had a pretty snug shack and I could lie there at night and hear the wind come howlin' down off the mountains.

This one day when I was out, I found an old mother coyote in a trap, and after I'd skinned her out, I noticed a cave with her tracks around it and signs of her comin' and goin'. Anyway, I scratched around and hauled out two little feisty pups.

Thinkin' they might be some company for the long winter evenings, I took 'em down to the shack. Turned out they were, too, as soon as they got used to me fussin' around.

One night when it was blowin' up a storm outside, I took out the old mouth organ and started to play. You should have seen the pups' ears perk up. Got half way through "Red River Valley" when one of 'em started to howl, and then the other. With me a-blowin' and them a-howlin', we were makin' quite a racket. 'Fore the evening was out, we had "Red River Valley" down pretty good—even had a kind of harmony. One howled tenor and the other almost soprano, and ever' now and then I'd stop blowin' and come in with a bass. Two nights later we had "Red River" down almost perfect—and then I switched tunes. Started to play "My Wild Irish Rose." The pups listened through once, and then on the next go-round they

joined in, and it wasn't long till they had that one too.

Seemed like they could hardly wait for me to come draggin' in each night. Always under my feet while I was cookin' supper or sweepin' out the shack, and always waitin' for me to reach for the old mouth organ. When we'd had our music, they'd be satisfied to curl up by the stove for the rest of the night.

First off, I thought it was pretty cute, them singin' and even carryin' a tune, but there come a time when things got out of hand. Like one night I had shucked down and was almost asleep, when back in the hills someplace the wild ones began their lonesome howlin'. 'Course my two pups answered with their music. Back and forth it went, first the wild yappin', then my two with one or the other song I'd taught 'em. This went on night after night till I thought I'd surely die from lack of sleep. Finally, when I couldn't stand it no longer, I grabbed both pups by their tails, flung 'em out in the snow, and went back to bed.

They hung around the shack whimperin' for a week or two, howlin' and yappin' those two tunes all night long. I didn't feed 'em or anything, and after a while they went away.

If you're ever passin' through Cedar Flats on an evening, stop and listen for the coyotes. If they're out and the wind is right,

they won't be howlin' like most you hear. They'll be singin'—and not just the two pups, but ever'one of them critters within forty miles. There'll be a regular chorus of "Red River Valley" or "My Wild Irish Rose"!

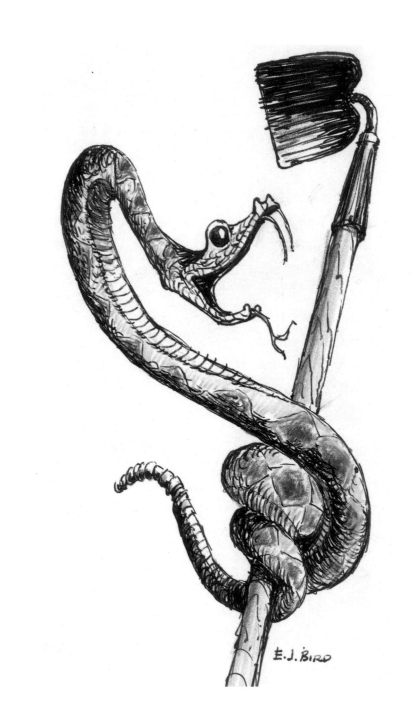

The Snake

Maw was always fussy about things around the ranch. Kept us busy all the time, plantin' and mowin', grubbin' and hoein', and things like that.

It was my turn at the garden, so this one mornin' real early, while the dew was on the grass, I took the hoe and started workin' on the string beans. Went down one row and started back on the second when the rattler struck! He sunk them old fangs into the hoe handle so far that it was hard to shake him loose. Rattlers are mean and ornery and full of poison.

Well now, that hoe handle started to
swell, and it swelled and swelled some
more. Got so big it wiped out all the string
beans, pushed out three rows of potatoes,
and wound up in the gooseberries before
she stopped. I tell you, that was quite a
log just layin' there in the garden. Anyway,
it took me and my dad and four brothers

three days to get her loaded and hauled down to the mill where they sawed her into lumber. Got enough to build a new bunkhouse.

After a couple of years, Maw was at it again. This time she wanted things painted up around the ranch. We did the house and the barn and the chicken coop and started on the bunkhouse. Must have been that the turpentine in the paint counteracted with the poison in the boards, 'cause the old bunkhouse started to shrink. Surprisin' how much she shrunk. We stood there and watched her go. Shrunk down to a little-bitty pile 'bout like a handful of toothpicks!

Fast Horses

We were sitting on our bedrolls, drinking coffee flavored with the ash from the sagebrush cookfire. All of us were staring out across the big country, each with his own thoughts.

One of the grandest sights in this world has to be sunset on the desert. That night it was as if Creation was making up to us for any drabness she may have left somewhere else. To the west the sky was fire-orange and yellow and gold, with the sun sending shafts of pale light between the darks of the ever-moving clouds. Far in the distance you could see the cliffs of the Fold, all clear-cut purples and blues, stacked like cardboard, range upon range, one behind the other.

Over there, beyond the valley, was a desert rainstorm, for all the world like a great broom hanging from the sky down to the earth. It swept the dust devils before it, traveling fast. Lightning lit up the clouds in bright orange flashes. Then you heard the thunder, far away, like great drums rolling, making echoes in the hills.

"How fast do the storms move?"

"About forty, fifty miles an hour," says Buck Lee, who's desert-born and knows such things. "Did I ever tell you about my fast team of horses?" Without waiting for an answer, he tells this story:

"Great team of matched bays, they was, prettier than two aces in five-card stud. White faces, and each with two front feet white from the knees down. Grain fed and

brushed shiny, hooked to a buckboard, they
was mighty high steppers, and most likely

the fastest two horses in the whole South-
west.

"Well, just about this time of an evening,
we was comin' across the desert, just amblin'
along with the buckboard movin' easy,
when I see behind me this rainstorm movin'
right up my back. Now them things travel,
as you can plainly see, and I wondered if
I could outrun it. I whipped up the bays

and headed for the ranch, with this rain
breathin' down my neck. You won't believe
this, but when we got to the barn, both
me and the horses was drier 'n a bone—
but the whole back end of the buckboard
was plumb full of water!"

The Splay-Footed Doe

Must have been in the early spring, 'cause I was trimmin' out the apple trees when I first saw the doe. Here she come, swimmin' across the river, just as brave as you please. She shook the water off and come a-trippy-toein' up through the orchard, strippin' the buds from the ends of the young branches— and she wasn't askin' could she do it, either.

I headed for the shack and got the old Winchester off the hooks in the kitchen, loaded her up, and sneaked back through the trees.

She just stood there and looked at me, and kept right on a-chewin'. I took a pretty good aim and pulled the trigger. Seems to me I hit her, but she just flitched her tail a little and went back to chewin' on the apple buds. I fired another round, and nothin' much happened, so I gave her six more and run plumb out of shells. And the

doe, finally, when she was full of buds, looked around and headed for the river, leavin' me with my mouth open, standin' there like a wind-blowed scarecrow.

Every day now we'd go through the same thing, with me bangin' away at her, and her chewin' on the trees. Figured it out once, cost me forty-two dollars and fifty-eight cents for shells alone, and the only thing I could see it was doin' was maybe makin' her splay-footed from carryin' all that lead around. Got to be kind of a game with me. I'd say to myself, "Just one more

time," and she'd flitch her tail again and go on rippin' at the apple trees.

All that summer she pestered me, takin' over the orchard like a mouse in a corn-crib—and somehow I just couldn't seem to get her off my mind. Then in the fall, it happened.

Here she come, swimmin' across the river. She wasn't skippin' around much by now. She was real heavy and slow-like and her tracks were deep and splayed. She walked up through the orchard and started munchin' on the apples, and I went and fetched the old gun. Then I said to myself, "Just one more time!"

She looked quite pitiful when I shot. Slow and careful, she ambled down towards the river, and as soon as she hit a deep place—she sunk plumb out of sight!

I always tell myself that it was that last bullet that sunk her. Or again, it could've been the apples she'd eaten, 'cause they get kind of heavy when they're wet.

Old Arlie

Me and old Arlie Peterson had been pros-
pectin' out in the Range Creek country
when this blizzard hit. Might say we was
lucky, 'cause we stumbled onto an old line-
camp cabin built years ago by the Blue Bell
ranch. Someone had stacked firewood by
the door, and we scratched around and
dragged some feed into the lean-to for the
two burros. 'Bout all we had to do then
was lay back and watch her blow.

I tell you, that was a storm. Laid down
two feet of snow the first night. The wind
was howlin' in off the flats and whistlin'

through the cracks, really bangin' things around. We was doin' all right till old Arlie started ailin'. Took t' coughin' and runnin' a fever hotter 'n a two-dollar pistol. All we had in the way of relief was a half-full jug of corn whiskey. I poured him some in a tin cup, then some more, and set there most of the night with him. I must have dozed off, 'cause when I come to, old Arlie was dead.

Couldn't believe it at first, but he was stone-cold dead! He wasn't breathin', no heartbeat, and his eyes were open, just starin' blank-like at the wall.

As much as I liked old Arlie, I couldn't help but feel sorry for myself. There I was, out in the hills, three feet of snow on the ground and more a-comin', and me with a dead man to worry about.

First two or three days, I had him laid out on the floor in a corner. Had him covered with a blanket and all, but it was kinda spooky in there with the cabin bein' so small. 'Long about the third night, I took him out into the lean-to and packed him all around with snow; thought he'd keep better that way. I knew somehow I had to get him back to town.

The storm kept on for two weeks or more. Nothin' but snow, the wind forever blowin', and it was cold and lonesome in the cabin. Got so bad I'd slip out and uncover old Arlie's face and talk to him just to keep from goin' crazy. I'd talk about the good times we'd had together, and all the people we both knew, and about the storm, things like that. Finally it let up some, and the sun leveled things off enough so I could travel.

Bein' awful stiff and hard to handle, I somehow got the body lashed to one of the burros. Had it tied to the pack saddle. Got all my gear together and headed down through the canyon toward town.

First night out I found me a box canyon, away from the wind. Plenty of dry cedar

about, so I soon had me a good fire goin'.
Had old Arlie unpacked and laid behind
me, wrapped in a blanket, all cold and stiff.
Without even thinkin', I started talkin' to
myself—you know how you do when you're
alone out there. You sing a little and mutter

41

somethin' under your breath. Finally I started talkin' to old Arlie.

"Arlie," I said, "this would have been a humdinger of a trip if you hadn't up and died on me."

"What do you mean, died on you?" asked Arlie.

"I mean back there at the cabin, when you—" Then it got to me, and I turned around. Old Arlie was settin' there, natural and calm as could be.

You can imagine how I felt with him talkin' away, and me not even bein' able to answer back. I just set there with my mouth open, starin' at him.

Old Arlie? Sure, he's alive; didn't even get frostbit. He's married and got four kids. Lives in a place down near the county seat. We get together quite often and talk about old times.

The Spotted Cow

I hear old Coalie Iverson's ailin'. He's goin' on eighty-five now, but he's a tough old turkey, and it's my guess he's still got a mile or two left in him. Years back, when we was both workin' for the old Bar-T, we had us some great times together. He was in his seventies then, all stove up with rheumatism and a bad back, but once in the saddle he was still a good hand.

This one time I remember, late in the fall, the boss sent the two of us out in the Rimrocks to fetch in some wild longhorns. The Rimrocks is mighty nasty country, with cut-up twisty canyons, mostly red rocks, and lots of prickly pear and rabbit brush. There's a mess of junipers and three days' good ride to any water. The cattle was wild as deer, never had a rope on 'em, and mean and ornery as the country itself.

We'd roped a few and had 'em penned

E.J. BIRD.

in a box canyon when we come upon this
old spotted cow. You could tell she was
old by the way she moved, and her horns
were long and crooked and scuffed up some
at the tips. She was skinny, but feisty as
a stomped-on rattler—and just about as
friendly. Coalie got a rope on her horns,

and she was givin' him a great ride out through the rocks and prickly pear till I snaked my rope on a back foot and throwed her. Had her stretched out there when Coalie got off his horse and went in for a closer look.

"I'll be a horned toad," he says. "This is the old Circle-P brand on her. If I remember right, it ain't been used for over fifty years! Let's look at her teeth," and we pried her mouth open and found she was a sure-enough gummer. "Lord-a-Mighty!" he went on. "If this old biddie was human, she'd be close to a hundred and thirty years old! She'll be tougher 'n a hame strap. I'm for turnin' her loose so's she can enjoy her last remainin' years."

I thought that was the end of it, but that night, after I'd been asleep for a couple of hours, old Coalie sets up in his bedroll and hollers, "I wonder what she eats? If I could find out, might cure this rheumatism or my back. Maybe I'd last another fifty years! I'm surely goin' t' find out in the mornin'."

Next day, while I'm out bustin' my tail draggin' in an old steer, Coalie was out slitherin' around through the brush, watchin' the spotted cow. He found out she et nothin' but these sour little blueberries that grow on the junipers, and he comes back to camp with a whole hatful.

"Wonder how's best to eat 'em?" He tried 'em raw and baked and fried and boiled.

Then he brewed 'em into a kind of thick tea—and he drunk about a quart.

Sometime along in the night I could hear him rattlin' around, moanin' and groanin' somethin' terrible. Then he tore out into the bushes and wandered back holdin' his belly. Worst case of Rocky Mountain Quick-Step I ever did see. Old Coalie thought sure he was goin' t' die, and before mornin', I thought so too. Nursed him three days before he could climb back in the saddle.

The other day I was out in the Rimrocks and happened to see the old cow again. She was still real sassy—kinda squared off when she saw me. Guess if I hadn't been horseback, she'd have chased me clear out of the county. Reminded me of old Coalie. Thought I might pick me a sack of those sour little berries and go up and see him.

Moonshine

Six, seven years ago I got to follerin' a two-bit rodeo. Figured I could make more in a summer 'n I could make at the ranch. This rodeo was run by old John Skinner, and we took in a bunch of the small towns in the north part of the state. Had a good string of buckin' stock and put on a passable show. I took a likin' to this one mare that John called Moonshine. I think he called her Moonshine because of her color, but the bronc riders had somethin' else in mind. Old back country sippin' whiskey and the mare both—you mess around with either one long enough and you'd surely be the loser in the end.

She was prettier 'n snow on the mountain, mostly white, with darker markin's on her legs and face. Liked to watch her come out of the chute, jumpin' all stiff-legged and bellerin' like a calf, no two jumps alike

E. J. BIRD

and all of 'em real bone-crushers. She'd go up higher 'n a scared magpie and swap ends. Never knew where she'd land. One time I saw her actually kick a feller's hat off, an' him settin' straight up in the saddle.

One thing about her though—she'd put on a great show, but when that whistle blew for time, she'd flat out stop buckin' and trot back to the holdin' pen.

Come that fall, old John decided to quit. He was tired of movin' every week, his back was hurtin', and besides, he said, he had it made. Started sellin' off the stock, and bein' I had a little day money saved, I up and bought the mare.

All that winter I worked with her and gentled her, and come spring she'd let me ride her without tossin' me sideways. Got so she liked ranch work and would whinny when I come into the barn. With me in the saddle and her long mane flyin', it was really somethin'. I felt almost like the head rooster.

This one mornin' it was rainin' a little, so I saddled her in the barn. I mounted up and reached down and unlocked the Dutch door. Guess she thought it was a buckin' chute, and she come out of there really flyin'. After two jumps she left me settin' high in the air, my arms and legs churnin' around like a rusty windmill. Well, she bucked all over the place, her a-snortin' and bellerin', and the saddle flyin' ever' which-a-way.

You know, she bucked till she died, right there 'long-side the barn. Wasn't nobody there to blow the whistle!

51

Cindy

Seen old Long Gone John down at the Chinaman's last night. He'd just polished off two big T-bones and was workin' on his third cup of coffee. He was settin' there, smilin' to hisself, smokin' a four-bit ceegar. Asked me to set with him a spell and keep him company. I could tell he wanted to talk—so I let him.

Seems as how he'd got a hankerin' to prospect out in the Big Blues, and after gettin' his outfit together, he bought two burros off'n Slim Sykes. Slim told him the

E.J. BIRD

gray was called the Prophet 'cause he would bray two hours before any rainstorm. Said the black was Cindy, after some gal he knew in Denver, and that Cindy was the smart one.

He'd been out a couple of weeks, he said, and everything old Slim had told him about the burros was right. That Prophet would bray every two hours, on the hour, every hour, day and night, whether it rained or not—and the racket was drivin' him out

of his mind. Cindy was smart enough to rummage through everything in camp till she found and et two pounds of bacon. He'd grabbed him a stick and pounded her tail some, and she went sulkin' off up the mountain.

Long Gone decided to move on. He'd found a little color in the creek, but not enough to hang around for. Old Prophet was easy. He got the pack on, then looked for Cindy. Finally found her up on the hillside in the shade of an old juniper, just standin' there switchin' her tail.

Stubborn-like, she set her feet when he tried to move her. He thought maybe she was still a-sulkin'. No matter what he did, she wouldn't budge. He pushed and he tugged and he finally dragged her a little with her feet plowin' up the ground. The way he told it, he was plumb tuckered out. Had to set there cussin' while he rested a minute. Just happened to look down, and right there where Cindy's feet had been

Cindy

draggin' he found it. She'd tore into a regular vein. Gold, sure as shootin'! Gold, layin' there, all bright and shinin' in the sun! That Cindy was much smarter 'n he'd thought.

After he'd filed his claim and done all things necessary, some feller from Texas come and bought him out. Long Gone made hisself quite a pile, the way he told it.

I asked him what he was doin' now. Said he'd bought the old Tate place, up near Hank's Holler, and had put forty acres into nothin' but clover. There's where he kept his burros—and he'd take old Cindy a pound of bacon every Sunday morning. Thought he might even go to Denver with the prospects of gettin' married.